Hello, Family Members,

Learning to read is one of the most important accomplishments of early childhood. **Hello Reader!** books are designed to help children become skilled readers who like to read. Beginning readers learn to read by remembering frequently used words like "the," "is," and "and"; by using phonics skills to decode new words; and by interpreting picture and text clues. These books provide both the stories children enjoy and the structure they need to read fluently and independently. Here are suggestions for helping your child *before*, *during*, and *after* reading:

Before

- Look at the cover and pictures and have your child predict what the story is about.
- Read the story to your child.
- Encourage your child to chime in with familiar words and phrases.
- Echo read with your child by reading a line first and having your child read it after you do.

During

- Have your child think about a word he or she does not recognize right away. Provide hints such as "Let's see if we know the sounds" and "Have we read other words like this one?"
- Encourage your child to use phonics skills to sound out new words.
- Provide the word for your child when more assistance is needed so that he or she does not struggle and the experience of reading with you is a positive one.
- Encourage your child to have fun by reading with a lot of expression . . . like an actor!

After

- Have your child keep lists of interesting and favorite words.
- Encourage your child to read the books over and over again. Have him or her read to brothers, sisters, grandparents, and even teddy bears. Repeated readings develop confidence in young readers.
- Talk about the stories. Ask and answer questions. Share ideas about the funniest and most interesting characters and events in the stories.

I do hope that you and your child enjoy this book.

—Francie Alexander
 Reading Specialist,
 Scholastic's Learning Ventures

TO JILL FROM DANIEL
TO DANIEL FROM JILL
AND TO POTATOES
OF GOOD WILL

Text copyright © 1999 by Daniel Pinkwater.
Illustrations copyright © 1999 by Jill Pinkwater.
All rights reserved. Published by Scholastic Inc.
SCHOLASTIC, HELLO READER! and CARTWHEEL BOOKS and associated logos
are trademarks and/or registered trademarks of Scholastic Inc.

Library of Congress Cataloging-in-Publication Data

Pinkwater, Daniel Manus, 1941-
    Big Bob and the magic Valentine's Day potato / by Daniel Pinkwater;
illustrated by Jill Pinkwater.
        p.   cm.— (Hello reader! Level 3)
    Summary: To liven up Valentine's Day in Mr. Salami's second grade class,
Big Gloria describes the imminent arrival of the Magic Valentine Potato.
    ISBN 0-590-63275-2
    [1. Valentine's Day— Fiction.   2. Schools — Fiction.   3. Humorous stories.]
I. Pinkwater, Jill, ill.   II. Title.   III. Series.
PZ7.P6335Bf   1999
[E] — dc21   98-42694
                                                       CIP
                                                        AC

10 9 8 7 6 5 4 3 2 1   9/9 0/0 01 02 03 04

Printed in the U.S.A.   24
First printing, January 1999

BIG BOB
AND THE MAGIC
VALENTINE'S DAY
POTATO

by Daniel Pinkwater
Illustrated by Jill Pinkwater

Hello Reader! — Level 3

SCHOLASTIC INC.

Cartwheel
·B·O·O·K·S·®
New York Toronto London Auckland Sydney

Mr. Salami Gives Us Our Orders

I am Big Bob, the second-biggest kid in the grade. Big Gloria is the first-biggest kid in the grade. She is my friend.

Our teacher is Mr. Salami. He used to be a race-car driver. He was also a jet pilot and a deep-sea diver. He is a good teacher.

Mr. Salami said, "Valentine's Day is coming. On this holiday, we make pretty cards and give them to people we like. These are called valentines. We will make valentines here in the classroom."

Big Gloria made a face.
"Boring," she whispered to me.

Mr. Salami went on, "Since we all like each other, we will make valentines for everybody. We will draw hearts. We will make pretty lace out of paper. We will use glue. We will use glitter. We will use scissors. We will also make Valentine's Day decorations for the classroom."

Big Gloria whispered to me, "This is not good enough."

I whispered back, "No. Mr. Salami is not enjoying this."

"His heart is not in it," Big Gloria whispered.

"We should do something," I whispered. "We should do something to make Valentine's Day better."

Something to Make It Better

Big Gloria raised her hand.
"Mr. Salami! Mr. Salami! Will the Magic
Valentine Potato visit us?"

"The Magic Valentine Potato?"
Mr. Salami asked.

"Yes! Will it come to our classroom?"

"I don't think I have ever heard of the Magic Valentine Potato," Mr. Salami said.

"You have never heard of the Magic Valentine Potato?" Big Gloria asked. "It comes on Valentine's Day. It brings valentines and potato chips to good children. Everybody knows that."

Big Gloria poked me with her elbow.

"Yes!" I said. "The Magic Valentine
Potato is like Santa Claus. It is a
friendly potato. It is magic."

"We want the Magic Valentine Potato
to visit!" Billy Thimble, a boy in the
class shouted.

"It will not be Valentine's Day without the Magic Valentine Potato!" Tina Tiny, a girl in the class shouted.

"We love the Magic Valentine Potato!" the whole class shouted.

"We will see," Mr. Salami said.

"Yaaay!" the whole class shouted.

Potato Valentines

After school, Big Gloria said, "Big Bob, Billy Thimble, and Tina Tiny, come to my house. We will make potato valentines."

"I don't know how to make potato valentines," Big Bob said.

"I will show you," Big Gloria said.

"I don't know how to make potato valentines," Tina Tiny said.

"I will show you," Big Gloria said.

"I don't know how to make potato valentines either," Billy Thimble said.

"I will show you all."

"Did you make up the Magic Valentine Potato?" I asked.

"Of course I made it up," Big Gloria said. "Mr. Salami needed my help. Valentine's Day will be much better now."

Gloria showed us how to make potato valentines. You take a potato and cut it in half. Then you draw a heart on the flat part of the potato and cut away everything that isn't the heart. You spread poster paint on a cookie sheet and dip the potato heart in the paint. Then you press the potato on a piece of paper — and there's a heart, printed on the paper!

Cool.

We made simple hearts. Then we made fancy hearts. Then we made little potato decorations to print around the edges. We made lots of valentines.

"There will be enough for everybody in second grade," Tina Tiny said.

"Look! Here are two rolls of pink toilet paper," Big Gloria said. "We can print a heart on every square of toilet paper."

"Why? Why should we print a heart on every square of toilet paper?" Billy Thimble asked.

"We will hang it all around the walls of our classroom," Big Gloria said. "It will look good."

Cool.

Big Gloria's mother gave us a snack.
The snack was potato chips.

How appropriate.

Our Plan

This was our plan. We would come to school early. We would get there before Mr. Salami. We would put potato-print valentines on everyone's desk. We would hang the potato-printed pink toilet paper all around the room.

Then we would go away and come back at the regular time. We would tell Mr. Salami that the Magic Valentine Potato had decorated the room.

It was a great plan.

Without a Hitch

In the morning we met at Big Gloria's house. We carried the potato valentines and the rolls of potato-printed toilet paper in a shopping bag. We got to school early. The school was locked!

Big Gloria pounded on the door.
Mr. Willie, the janitor, came.

"School is not open yet," Mr. Willie said.

"Mr. Willie, we have to get in early,"
Big Gloria said. "We have to decorate
our classroom. It is a surprise."

Mr. Willie said, "Okay, Gloria. I will
let you in."

"It is also a secret," Big Gloria said.

"I understand," Mr. Willie said.

We went inside.

"Gloria, what if Mr. Willie had not let us in?" I asked.

"Ha!" Gloria said. "I knew he would."

"How did you know?"

"He is my uncle," Big Gloria said.

We went to the empty classroom. We put potato valentines on every desk. We put one on Mr. Salami's desk. We hung the potato-printed pink toilet paper, with a heart on every square, all around the room.

It looked great.

"Our plan worked without a hitch," Big Gloria said.

Potato Surprise

We came back with the rest of the class.

"Look at our classroom!" the other kids said.

"It looks great!"

"It looks cool!"

"The Magic Valentine Potato must have been here!" I said.

"Yes! It must have been the Magic Valentine Potato!" Billy Thimble said.

"The Magic Valentine Potato! The Magic Valentine Potato!" all the kids shouted.

We looked around for Mr. Salami. He was not there.

"This is unusual," Big Gloria said.

"Where is Mr. Salami?" Tina Tiny asked.

"Mr. Salami will be late," a voice said.
"But I am here."

"Who said that?"

"Who is that?"

"What is that?"

There was someone in the doorway.
It was someone or something.

"Look!" Billy Thimble shouted.

"Look!" Tina Tiny shouted.

"Oh my goodness!" I shouted.

"It's . . . ," Big Gloria shouted.

"It's the Magic Valentine Potato!" the whole class shouted.

And it was. It had to be. It couldn't have been anyone else. He was like a potato. He was dancing around the room. He gave us valentines and little bags of potato chips.

"I thought you made him up," I told Big Gloria.

"I thought I did, too," Big Gloria said.

"But look!" I said.

"Yes, look!" Big Gloria said.

"Yes, children, I am the Magic Valentine Potato," the Magic Valentine Potato said. "I am here to wish all of you a happy Valentine's Day and give you potato chips."

"Yaay!" the class shouted. "We love you, Magic Valentine Potato."

"I will go now," the Magic Valentine Potato said. "Mr. Salami will be here soon. Eat your potato chips and be good children."

"Good-bye, Magic Valentine Potato!" the class shouted. "We love you!"

The Magic Valentine Potato danced out of the room.

His Car Wouldn't Start

In a little while, Mr. Salami came in.

"I am sorry I am late," Mr. Salami said. "My car wouldn't start. Look at all the nice valentines! And you all have little bags of potato chips."

"Mr. Salami! Mr. Salami! The Magic Valentine Potato was here!" the class shouted.

"Really?" Mr. Salami asked. "Imagine that!"